BLACK-THROATED BLUE WARBLER

A NOVELLA

JORDAN SPALDING

Black-Throated Blue Warbler

J. S. Spalding

Bsky.app/profile/jpspalding.com on BlueSky,

Edited by Joni Di Placido
<u>www.PageandProof.com</u>

-

-

Front Cover designed by Megan Miller
https://www.etsy.com/shop/WasThatAnAardvark

 Formatted with Vellum

To Megan
For braving the wilderness to discover the nugget of
this story and suffering each new draft with grace.

And YAPY
for being a Black-Throated Blue Warbler in the right
place at the wrong time so we could marvel at you and
write stories about your life.

BLACK-THROATED BLUE
WARBLER

by Jordan Spalding

Disclaimer: In service of the story, some creative changes to birds' mental aptitudes, biology, and behavior were necessary. This is not a scientifically rigorous bird guide, nor should it be used as one.

1

MIGRATION

Warm Caribbean waters glittered, undulating beneath the balmy, tropical air. The moon's visage shattered into a million flickering fractals upon the sea's surface. The reflection gave no clue to the moon's fullness, except by the total illumination piercing that warm night. Sea spray danced through the air like a welcoming mister on an especially hot summer day; such a day had just concluded. An unusually warm, 82-degree, early spring was upon them. Despite the calendar marking late winter, the islands were ready for change. It was time.

The members of the strange sisterhood of the sky found themselves in precisely the middle of nowhere. And still they were, all of them, confident of their direction. Without a single shoreline visible on any horizon, the tiny murmuration flitted in a sort of unison through the air. Chirps echoed high above the foamy wash. To an untrained ear they sounded indistinguishable. A myriad of interchangeable, high-pitched *cheeps* resonating short distances, before submitting to the churning night-foam and squall. But in the intended earholes—finely attuned by a million years of evolution—they rang clear.

Some signaled their position, *"I'm here! I'm here!"*; some called out for a response from the others, *"Where are you? Where are you?"*. Some cried out a warning; a dangerous, impending swell rising to the level of their migratory altitude: *"Watch out! Watch out!"*. Others signaled the sighting of an occasional lone migrator passing by: *"Who's there? Who's there?"*. To which the answer was of course one of those powerful, long-winged shorebirds that would fly for several days nonstop, its silhouette dutifully engraved upon the fullness of the night's moon. Collectively, the chirps made up the healthy discourse of a migrating flock. Something to pass the hours between stopovers for rest and refuel. Necessary small talk to settle the restless nerves brought on by the perils of their crossing.

One bird fluttered reserved at a quiet edge of the flock. She was a Black-Throated Blue Warbler—a 'Blue' if you like—a pale, olive bird with buff undersides; narrow, white eyebrows; and a small, square, white wing patch called a 'handkerchief'. She was a small, insect-eating bird highly specialized to a diet of forest floor arthropods. She was middle-aged for her species, just shy of three years old. She did not have a name. To herself, she was simply herself and her mate had been her mate, and her fledgling offspring of last year were... a failure. (Not unusual for Warbler parents in their first year. Still learning the ropes and seeking out a better habitat.) Beyond that her social circle stopped. All others were simply the 'other'.

She did not have the mental chops of her distant cousins the Raven or the Parrot to handle complex social groups. And if she looked in the mirror, she would merely see a female of her own species. There, recognition would stop—even if someone had painted a red dot on her forehead, she would not attempt to wipe it away.

She mostly kept to herself... except during the Mating Season, and Migration. Other birds might enjoy the company of strangers through the winter, but she certainly did not. In this mixed flock, she'd scarcely interacted with anybody—beyond an annoyed chirp when someone got too close. (Even under the full moon this was a common problem, but the rules etched into the genetics of all of them told them migration happened at night.) They managed as well as they could, and so far, she had managed to keep to herself—

Except that the Hermit Thrush to her left kept staring at her ankle. Its bulbous, black eyes were optimized for the low light. And now they were sharply focused on the alternating silvery metal and brightly colored plastic bands that jangled around the Blue's legs. She tried to ignore the prying eyes, but they were just so large, and the Thrush would not look away.

"What are those things?" The Thrush chirped. The Blue did her best to pretend she didn't hear. The Thrush was after all just a harmless understory feeder whom she could afford to ignore. A fellow insectivore, but a world apart from any Warbler. With its barrel chest, stubby wings and long straight bill, the Thrush was adapted to feed on worms and burrowing bugs. To her, it appeared gangly and misshapen. Totally un-Warbler-like in its proportions; far too large. Though the Blue found most birds to be far too large.

Although they had spent the entire winter in the same coastal stretch of tropical forest, they had scarcely acknowledged each other's presence. Each was just one individual among thousands. A diaspora of small, foraging birds; all specialized and stratified to their niche. Their tree, their allotment of undergrowth, their target prey. (Why waste time when you could be looking for grubs in the undergrowth?) But at this very moment—when food was on no one's mind, and the act of flight was tediously rote—one couldn't help but look around. And unlike her presently obnoxious and misshapen neighbor, she was unable to fully hide the tiny hint of silver tucked in her belly feathers. That made her what she feared most: a topic for conversation.

"Is it hard to fly with those things on your legs?" *Ugh.*

"No. They're nothing" She harshly chirped back. She meant for the chirp to be harsh but also, as a Warbler, her chips were higher in pitch and sharper than those of the melodious Thrush. The Thrush, flapping only once for every three flaps the Blue made, stretched out her own—bizarrely long—legs. These were extremities well suited to dashing across a forest floor. *She looks so odd.* The Blue couldn't help but stare in turn. Each leg was nearly the length of the warbler's entire body. *Freak.*

The Thrush gestured to its feet— "I myself had scaly mites last season. A nasty thing. Cumbersome—"

"It's not Mites!" She blurted, exasperated at the Thrush's persistence.

She had no idea what scaly mites were exactly, (The inherent 'grotesqueness' of the phrase itself gleaned for her its assumed meaning in her mind) although she'd seen ghastly growths on other Blues before. Usually such deformations were a death sentence. In her brief experience she had seen only one 'unfit' individual make it longer than a few weeks post-affliction. That lone survivor suffered a skin rash and dropped several body feathers that season. He persisted however, relegated to the outer edge of another male's territory. He foraged and sang but failed to draw a mate. *She* had certainly avoided him.

Being different was not a good thing. That very sentiment was the driving force behind her squeamishness around her own unusual adornments. And yet there was something else about them that had always possessed her mind. They weren't infections or abnormalities; they were hers alone. They were the great secret she held.

Another voice chimed in "Where'd ya find 'em shinies? Come now, ain't no secrets 'n yander migration!" A hulking Ovenbird settled between them, flapping madly as it steadied itself. Although it looked similar to the Thrush, bulky and barrel-chested, it was actually a Warbler like herself; its long needle-like beak specialized for small flying insects. Bright black-and-orange stripes adorned its head and appeared glossy in the pale moonlight.

"Ya get stuck in spider silk? I suffered that ma'-self this season—"

The Thrush retorted, "Does that look like any kind of silk to you? More like—"

"Mites." the jittery Ovenbird nodded knowingly.

"It's not mites! Or silk! It's—it's none of your business!" She tried to maneuver away from the two bulky, pale brown birds but they were both above her now, and she wasn't a very strong flier. To drop lower meant getting dangerously close to the choppy waters—so she stayed put.

"A wersp o' silk got plumb wrap'd on ma' tail. An' right as the first fell free, 'nother un took its place! Off n' on, I was silk'd half the season if you'd believe it," drawled the Ovenbird.

"On account of all your bobbing I'd think. Tail-bobbing I mean. You folk can't sit still." The Thrush responded matter-of-factly.

"... That's exactly what happened—how'd you know that?"

The Hermit answered, "All you Ovens are the same. I've seen one, I've seen 'em all. Of a poorly tempered ilk but somehow free of any shame for it! Not a one willing to introspect on that poor condition which bedevils your kind. Jittery as squirrels and unfit for flocking—though who would listen to me on the subject? I, who's suffered countless hours watching from my lofty vantage the ways of the Oven—your fitful leaps from the underbrush—like prey pursued and like the pursuer all in one. A devastating, spasmodic disturbance to the otherwise unbroken peacefulness of our winter escape."—overriding the Ovenbird's attempt to interject, "Strikingly out of place amidst the harmony otherwise uninterrupted. I'm sure you'd agree if only you had carefully fostered an *objective* viewpoint, as I have." The Hermit Thrush and Ovenbird were fully ignoring the troubled maneuverings of the Blue beneath them; embroiled in their new contention.

"Well, I wouldn't claim that's—"

The Ovenbird pondered for a moment. Or rather, it stopped talking and focused chiefly on flying straight while a blank look overtook it. The overwhelmingly rich elitism of the Thrush's conviction had short-circuited the Oven's mind and he took a moment to recover. "I resent such a charct'sation-"

"If there's one thing I've learned about Ovens", The Thrush interrupted with a summary she had clearly just formulated as if to bring the discussion to a close, "is they bob and sway and can't stop. Even when it'd do them some good. Me? I've got self-control. I even beat a bad bout of scaly mites last season. Nasty, nasty thing."

The Ovenbird realized it in fact had no statement to disprove this sweeping generalization about its kind, beyond a vague feeling that that couldn't be right. And that part of the discussion did seem to be over, so it let its mind (and its flight path) drift back towards the annoyed little Blue in their midst. Thus, their mini flock ebbed and bobbed erratically as it resettled into a new equilibrium.

"Yander's the strangest silk I laid eyes on, lil'

lady. The strangest! An' I'm nearly five winters on these shores—" The Blue narrowly avoided being knocked by Oven. She regained her bearings and looked daggers at both her unwanted companions.

"It's a lack of self-control, in fact. Never once have I found myself tangled in anything like that. Mind you the scaly mites were hardly my fault. It was the result of an ill-fated rendezvous, if you must know."

"If I can't get you two to leave me alone and if you insist on labeling my trinkets,"— she took a deep breath and sighed. Such a feat was only possible because of the complex multi-chamber lungs of her kind. Any small songbird could manage both these things at the same time, the result being an intentional amplification of one's fed-up-ness.

—"Then I'll tell you, but I don't expect either of you will believe me, because it's like nothing any of you have ever seen, even if you've got five winters or ten! I doubt your poor Ovenbird will even be able to follow what I'm about to tell you." She waited for their assent.

"He's not *my* Oven. And I may not have seen as many winters as he, but I've seen every corner of the islands and I doubt anything you've got can surprise me." The Thrush puffed out her already barreled chest proudly.

The Blue chirped in hushed tones, her head held low as if she didn't want others of the mixed flock to hear. She certainly did not.

She whispered, "I was chosen." Slowly she extended her left leg. The first to appear around it was a silvery band stamped with strange symbols. The symbols were English characters—numbers and letters—but not even the combined brain power of the three conspirators could have deduced that fact. The second band, resting above the silvery one was a different material; plasticky, and bright-yellow colored. Bright enough to make a Yellow-Shafted Flicker blush. The whistling night air spun the two bands about her leg. They danced and bucked, their hollow rattle barely audible above the surf and the flock.

"What do you mean, 'chosen'? These strange things, they chose you?" asked the Hermit Thrush as incredulously as it could muster.

"No no, chosen as in... well, taken really. I was taken. These were the trinkets they left behind. They don't hurt, I hardly notice them now but—" she laughed to herself. Carefully, so she didn't lose control of her flight, she unsheathed her other leg, freeing it from her belly feathers. The group collectively gasped. Two more bands! Both plastic. One as pink as a Spoonbill and the other as yellow as the blushing Flicker on her left. The Ovenbird was transfixed. His black-and-orange crest involuntarily jolted upward; a sign of alarm and intense interest in his species. Bobbing indeed.

"They sure are sumtin', them shinies. But things bein' as they are, migration an' all, I'd just soon be leaving 'em behind? If 'twere up to me."

"Fool! You think I haven't tried?" The Blue snapped at the Oven. She eyed them both seriously and said, "They may hang freely now, but they'll never get over my toes, see?" She jangled the bands. They bounced against her closed foot. Even in the tumult of free-flying migration, it was clear they would not come off easily.

"They're lightweight and hardly a bother I suppose; sometimes I go days without noticing they're even there. But I've pecked at them for endless hours, and they are truly unbreakable. Made of some substance like I've never known."

The Thrush spoke, "I've seen a substance like that. Shiny and unbreakable. In that big Human-Territory in the middle of the island. Great blocks of the stuff in every shape."

"Ain't never been to the Human-Ter't'ry, though I know of it," remarked the Ovenbird.

"The same." Said the Blue, "I've never had cause to leave the woods. I've heard there's nothing for us forest birds there...."

"It's true, it's a barren place. I've found some bugs but—there are many more hazards, and too many of those ungracious Weaver Finches. With their thick accents that you can't make heads or tails of, and they're bullies the whole lot of them. A dangerous place. But as I've told you, I've seen every bit of these islands."

The Weaver Finch the Hermit was referring to, was of course the omnipresent House Sparrow. An aggressive, capable and adaptive invasive species. The Blue shuddered quietly, thinking of them.

It wasn't as unusual as it seemed that the Hermit Thrush found herself deep in the human territory. It wasn't unheard of for birds to get lost during migration, end up somewhere half-suitable and decide to stay. Sometimes you found a place totally unlike your expected destination, and a far better habitat overall. Even if none of your kind were present, it was a small price to pay for a sizable and uncontested bounty. Sometimes the very absence of any others of your kind was the root cause of the plentiful nature of a new place. There was some value in heading off the beaten path from time to time, though the risks were high. Such happy accidents were even passed down to offspring, occasionally.

"Are there trinkets like these in the Territory?" The Blue asked the Thrush with genuine curiosity.

"No no, but the material is familiar to me. I'm possessed of unparalleled perception; you can take me at my word. These are one in the same."

She ignored the Thrush's boasting, "It doesn't matter anyway, I didn't get these on the island, I got them in the Abenaki Hills."

To the human denizens of New Hampshire, the region the Black-Throated Blue Warbler was talking about was known as White Mountains National Forest, but of course the birds only knew the indigenous name.

"Abenaki! The summer nesting grounds," Chirped the Ovenbird, his crest peaking in excited recognition. "Our very destination!"

"You're saying you've carried these... *things* all the way from Abenaki to the islands and now back? They've stayed on you more than a full season?" spat the Thrush in disbelief.

The Blue continued, "The... beings that chose me made sure of it. I remember them clasping the trinket around my leg. Mind you I was just a nestling, barely six days old. Mother was calling for us to leap to safety. A few of my siblings had already done so, but they got me before I could escape...." She paused deep in thought, "My eyes were barely open then, but I could just manage to make out some giant shape, like a beak of a Hawk or Heron. It came down, with the trinket in its maw. I wriggled and squirmed in every way I knew how but something held me fast." Her audience was frozen in rapt attention.

"I watched that great and nightmarish beak grasp my leg. I braced for the pain of the bite but... somehow it didn't even touch me. It enveloped my leg in a perfect fitted gap, then it unsealed, leaving behind the trinket. Everything happened in an instant. Like it had been designed for this very purpose. For me."

"Oh my, oh my...." The Ovenbird looked at both the Blue's trinkets, breathless with wonder. The Blue retracted them back under her belly feathers and steadied her flight.

The Hermit Thrush remained unimpressed, "Pshah, ridiculous! I had no idea you Warblers could conjure such a fantastic story just to avoid the embarrassment of getting your foot caught on something! Why don't you just find a Grosbeak to bite it off for you?"

"That's the thing! I'm not the only one with these trinkets. The only other bird I've ever met with one similar was a Grosbeak. Only he just had the silver one."

"Did ya ask 'em where he got 'em?"

The Blue recoiled, slightly embarrassed, "No I... I try to keep to myself. Still, I did watch him for a great while, before he disappeared," she admitted.

"I bet he chewed off the colored trinkets already. Only the silver he couldn't break."

"Maybe he did. The colored trinkets certainly have more..." she searched for the right word, "pliancy to them."

The Hermit Thrush seemed pleased with herself. "That'd square with my understanding of such human substances as I've seen in their territory—"

The Ovenbird interrupted, "—Or he only had the one? Maybe not all garn'r the colors you carry. Maybe not all are *worthy*?"

"Oh hush fool, you're clearly out of your depth." The Hermit Thrush shushed the Oven. The Oven looked curiously down at the churning surf, checking his altitude.

"All the more reason to know I was chosen." the Blue added quietly.

"*Chosen*, Ha! Meaningless drivel! A simple mind like yours is predisposed to such ethnocentrism, I know. But the world is bigger than you, my dear Warbler!" the Thrush snapped.

"You've spent too long with those unseemly Weaver Finches I think. It sullied your mood. I always thought Hermit Thrushes were cheerful beings with your beautiful songs—"

"We are not all the same, little Warbler. Some are cheerful, some mean, some as empty-headed as our Oven-friend. Besides it is the males that sing. I have heard many of their songs in the Abenaki Hills and maybe a simple Blue like you is indiscriminately awed, but I am not so easily impressed."

The Oven, satisfied that he was in fact in his depth with respect to the cruising height of the flock, returned to the conversation, "What's it that bein' 'chosen' garn'rs ya? Do you come across more morsels fer less foragin'? Or are yer nestlings more hearty n' vigorous than the neighbor's?"

"No no, nothing like that. It's hard to explain... or, well—well, the truth is I don't know yet." she confessed. The Thrush snorted. She continued, "But I'm patient. I'm sure it'll reveal itself when it's time. Whatever it may be."

The Thrush pointed to the bands poking out of the Blue's belly feathers, "Looks like Human meddling if you ask me. They're like a pack of unruly crows, doing things for no reason, making an unnecessary ruckus."

"I told you you wouldn't believe me," said the little Blue, resigned.

"Humans ain't a thing like crows. I've seen 'em. They don't even fly. Least not I've seen in ma five winters ...." The Ovenbird trailed off as the Hermit Thrush veered away from the two Warblers, muttering something about an 'utter waste of time'. With that, their tenuous mini flock broke up. The Oven watched the retreating Thrush for a time before turning back to the Blue. The Blue had secretly hoped he'd follow the Thrush and leave her alone. She already felt thoroughly embarrassed at the reception her revelation had received.

"I believe ya, lil' lady. That's a great obligation

ya carry an' I dunnit envy you. Good winds t'ya."
With that the Oven retracted its crest and hobbled
on unsteady wings further up in the flock. Several
smaller birds swerved to avoid the rising Oven.

Once the Ovenbird had faded into the masses
of the flock, there was a spell of silence. The night
air carried a quiet whistle between the tensed
feathers of the Blue's wings. She let out a breath
and loosened the tightness in her chest she hadn't
even been aware of. The incessant prying audience had dispersed, and she was left to peer out
into the darkness.

The gentle shift of the earth's electromag-
netism stimulated the chromatophores in her
eyes, updating her visual perception of the geo-
magnetism. Like a pair of glasses revealing the
contours of earth's field, the chemical change
pressed in her mind a sensation utterly alien to
anyone who was not a bird: but comfortingly familiar to her. Its gentle tug was pleasantly warm.
She waited, letting it gradually build in its insis-
tence, the force growing and ebbing slowly, slowly.
Finally she let it overtake her and she course-cor-
rected—and unconsciously felt the bulk of the
murmuration around her roughly match the
change in heading. This great order of life, those
who flew on favorable winds could take for
granted the miracle of their specialized head
organ that aligned them to the great geomagnet-
ism. A gift as great as seeing time or tasting the
intentions of the earth herself. The very tool that
made this genetically predestined night migration
possible in the first place.

Peeking through the darkness like a ghostly

silhouette, the Black-Throated Blue Warbler spied their next stopover cresting the horizon along with the sunrise. It was Noepe, known to its non-indigenous occupants as Martha's vineyard. They were on the last leg of their journey. By this time tomorrow she'd be back home in the Abenaki Hills. This year she was determined to get a nest that would make it. She already had the perfect spot in mind.

2

ABENAKI

She had completed another full day of flight out from Noepe by the time she reached her destination. The Blue dropped below the cloud layer and saw the old familiar land stretching out before her. The Abenaki Hills was a densely shifting morass nestled deep in the mountains of the new world. Great rolling mountains carpeted by unbroken forest top. It looked as if it went on forever, fading into the humid, foggy mist of the east coast spring air.

Shadowy and cool, the thicket was at maximum abundance. Every fixed atom of Nitrogen was wrapped up in service to a plant, then an animal, then a fungus, then the soil, then a plant again. Over four hundred plant species called it home, but a few of them dominated.

She looked down, more detail resolving itself now. Below her was a patchwork of trees, all competing for the limited canopy. A visible struggle that mirrored the invisible beneath the soil; the thick knotted matrix of intertwined roots dutifully lapping up every available nutrient in the loamy depths. Stands of silky, knotted beech clustered together in impenetrable garrisons. Sinewy sugar maples spiraling upward.

Some of the maples had curious, prominent twists and right angles in their growth, as if a giant had absentmindedly stepped on them while passing through. Two hundred years prior, these tortured trees had been patiently twisted by indigenous peoples to serve as conspicuous waypoints to their descendants. Today, they remain devotedly contorted for no one but the birds of the quiet forest.

Countless papery-white birch trees shined like beacons, dotting the shadowy thicket. They were tall and skinny; all their energy stores reaching heavenward and almost none invested in their circumferences. Compared to the other trees, their lives were brief and hectic. Compared to a Warbler, they were eternal.

The little Blue hovered over the patches of trees; subtle visual cues informing her direction. She dropped below the canopy, still searching for home. Deep in the forest, the Wood Ferns jutted out from every nook and cranny. They fanned out their ancient—yet still well-adapted—forms like a delicate integument over the whole of the forest floor. Each one enfolding moisture in its forever-uncoiling new growth.

Thick bouts of hobblebush filled the middle-spaces from the ground up to a few meters high. Its large, bulbous leaves furnished layers and layers of cover. The underside of nearly every leaf concealed a diverse menu of arthropods. There were spiders, crane flies, and lepidoptera (the last in their incipient, caterpillar forms). These made up the juicy morsels that would fuel this year's Blue families.

In the vast old-growth forest, nearly as many trees had fallen and were rotting on the forest floor. Hundreds of once-proud trunks gave up their pulpy interiors to the open air. Brown and starchy, steaming hot from the ceaseless duties of bacteria and mycelial networks. Ready-made baby food for the saplings erupting from the carcass. Such were the cycles of life unabated.

She stopped for a drink at a dribble of water. All around her, a smattering of moss-covered boulders—smoothed by a thousand years of trickling water—covered sections of forest floor. Thin lines of fresh mountain stream snaked through, carving a path down the watershed. A thick layer of fallen leaves in various stages of decomposition covered this bedlam, this *Life*. The truth of the old growth was there was no 'floor'. That would be too orderly, too frozen in time. The forest was an unevenly treacherous, spongy carpet, barely traversable by large mammals and utterly perfect for small songbirds. Especially those who nested low to the ground like the Black-Throated Blue Warbler.

She landed on the lowest branch of the towering beech and let out a great sigh of relief. She had high site-fidelity and wouldn't have felt truly at home till she had landed on this exact tree. The moment her feet touched the gnarled, hard-wood branch it triggered a dormant memory. Her mother pecking at the new trinkets strapped to her skinny legs: fussing with them in between feedings. She surveyed her home with a practiced fervor. The rains had been heavy and relentless this year. She cocked her head sideways. A bright pinprick of red-orange caught her eye from far below. In the precious-little clearing through the hobble, she spied an Eft. One of the forest's stranger inhabitants; the tiny salamander was barely two centimeters long. But it was striking! She noted that the amphibian was uniformly the color of the inside of a blood orange (with a light peppering of black spots), and its skin was the texture of the outside of one. It ambled by at an extremely casual pace. Without fear of predation or demands of any obligation. The Eft emanated a relaxed familiarity with the forest.

The Blue couldn't know it, but it was a familiarity well-earned. The little creature had been wandering amongst the rotting leaves for longer than the Blue had been alive. And it would keep wandering for several more years, fulfilling this leg of its peculiar lifecycle before finally returning to its aquatic stage as a proper newt. Lacking the hectic, fast paced nature of the Blue's world, they had virtually nothing in common. They lived, for all practical purposes, in entirely different realities. And yet, she couldn't help but watch the creature as it ambled out of sight under a large, sagging hobble leaf. The world was indeed larger than herself, with countless ways of being. She was learning that more every day.

Zoo-Zoo-Zweeeee! Zoo-Zoo-Zoooo-Zweeeeee!

Her head snapped up at the sound of the familiar song. A male Black-Throated Blue Warbler proclaiming its territory and calling out to any prospective females. So it was finally happening. Her thoughts of migration and salamanders and her fledgling days were tucked away for later musings. She shook off the funk of her former self. A calling greater than her closely held secret overcame her all at once. She was experiencing the inescapability of nature.

Already her breast feathers twinged with inevitability—preparing to fall out and create her bare-bellied brood patch (A more effective direct skin contact to help keep the eggs warm). Other changes marched forward with a steady certainty, hidden behind her fluff and below even her own conscious awareness. Her alternative plumage already began sprouting across her head and back. A yearly ritual of all songbirds coinciding with the mating season. The various shades of brown that made up her complexion today wouldn't dramatically change with this transformation. She would never molt into the showy aqua-blue and tar-black of the males of her species (the source of their namesake), but she would spend her spring and summer in her best coat. Fresh, bright and glossy plumes shown starkly against her tattered migration-feathers of last year's molt. There was one proud focal point; her 'handkerchief'—the striking white square on a Blue's wing, present on males and females. It was situated on the base of her primary feathers (closest to the coverts), and shone brighter than a dollop of opal. Her elegance would leave no doubt of her bountiful winter in the Caribbean. This year's La Niña had been kind to many species near the equator, and she had found the forests of Xaymaca lousy with small arthropods.

Even her brain was undergoing mysterious seasonal changes. It had grown nearly ten percent since the early warm weather had first roused her instinctual programming. A larger brain meant better foraging, and survival. But it also meant better discernment between male songs. She would soon be up to the task of distinguishing the territories, health, and intent of the numerous raucous calls of prospective suitors. Of course, the real magician's trick was collating these data points to predict who among them would be the best in rearing their offspring. And that was, of course, impossible to know. She learned that last year.

Nevertheless, equipped with her superior intelligence and her glossy coat, she felt confident in her chances. She knew this year would be different.

3

THE MALE

Zoo Zoo Zweeee! Zoo Zooo Zoooooo Zweeee!

It was a strong call. A healthy call. She spied him darting through the upper canopy. A vibrant and glossy male who hopped from branch to branch, surveying his territory. She waited for him to drift closer to her. His territory, it seemed, contained the beech tree she had sat on as a fledgling so long ago. As a female she didn't need to hold a territory herself, though she considered the visible radius surrounding her beech to be 'hers' as much as anything in the forest.

Zooooo Zoooo-

The male stopped, cocking his head down towards her. She rousted—the equivalent of a satisfied shudder—fluffing herself and straightening any errant feathers. She took flight and landed on a thick birch a few meters away. Still within line-of-sight of the curious male. She faced away from the male and preened herself. She acted absentminded, as if she had not seen or heard the male (though her preening was tense and she worked more quickly than she would have liked). The male bounded to a high branch on the opposite side of the birch, well within her view—

Zoooo Zoooo Zoooo Zweeeeeeeeee!

His entire body heaved in the intensity of the call. It was twice as loud as the territory call she had first noticed, and he displayed his glossy black throat proudly. She turned away from him again but did not fly away. She stole a glance over her shoulder.

The male fluttered to her branch, taking the invitation. He landed and inspected her from a safe distance so as to not chase her off. His head bobbed to and fro.

She stood perfectly still. She pretended to be engrossed in a knot in the branch, but her tensed feet said otherwise. Her already fast heartbeat quickened.

The male turned sideways displaying his flank. He flattened out his body with his wings and fluttered them slightly. He cocked his head to one side, curious, and dared to bound a centimeter closer. She matched his hop a centimeter further away.

Zooooo Zooooo Zoooooo Zwwweeeeeee!

Her heart fluttered. For a moment she wanted to fly away, overwhelmed by the intensity of the male calling right next to her. But for the first time, she turned and took him in. Although it was early in the season, she felt ready. She hopped a centimeter closer to the male.

The male's eyes darted down. They looked at her legs where her trinkets jangled and settled from her hop. The male turned to face the odd artifacts head-on. No longer displaying but looking with curiosity and... something else.

He hopped closer. She held her breath—but something was different. The male was focused on her legs. Too focused. She spun a hundred and eighty degrees in a single hop to show her other flank. Her 'handkerchief' shone brightly in the morning sun. It was her best side.

The male inched closer, crouched with his face close to her ankles now. *What was he doing?*

She looked at him with a mixture of annoyance and hesitation. Surely if he had come this close, he was interested. He was the most striking male she had ever seen. She began to worry about how he would take her ornaments. Should she try to explain herself? That hadn't turned out so well in the migration flock, but then again virtually none of those other birds had been Blues. Maybe he would understand, maybe he'd seen it before in these hills?

Being different was not a good thing. She reminded herself. The male tensed, millimeters from her as if frozen in indecision.

"They're um—" she started. Poke. He prodded one of the bands with his bill. Then the other. Poke, poke. The male stepped back and looked at her curiously again. No, suspiciously. She couldn't believe he'd just poked at her! Like some forgettable novelty. Things were going so well and now.... Now she was almost disgusted at his behavior. But maybe they could still repair the situation. Recapture the mood. She waited for him to ask her the question that everyone asked her. She was silent, better to wait for him to make the first move.

He hopped another centimeter back, facing away from her now. The male looked back at her one last time with some impenetrable emotion on his face and then—leapt from the branch and flew off back towards the heart of his territory. He hadn't even bothered to ask. From fighting for her attention to leaving without a word.

Zooo Zooo Zwweeee!

Distantly he picked up his song again. She sighed, dejected. *That was it*, she guessed. He would not talk to her again. For a female to pursue a male was unheard of. If only she had explained herself! Had she not told countless nosy birds her story? Could she not summarize it eloquently enough by now to be properly understood? To reason with a male of her own species? Perhaps his shiny black mask had caught her voice in her throat. Perhaps she had assumed foolishly that her trinkets would be seen as some sort of colorful accessory. That they would not be seen as disease or disfigurement. Clearly, she was wrong.

Her stomach growled, wrenching her from her self-deprecating line of thinking. She tried to forget the male for the moment and threw herself completely into the hunt. She landed on a beech sapling and peered at the underside of each leaf for her quarry. The world of the forest took these fleeting interactions of the Warblers in stride. It was all part of the natural cycles. Her relentless foraging strengthened the bloodlines of the lepidoptera through natural selection. Even if the lepidoptera hardly appreciated her efforts. Moths transmuted into Warbler. And her nest the previous year fed a struggling family of Blue Jays against her best efforts. Warbler transmuted into Jay. And the Blue Jay buried hundreds of beech nuts that fell. They forgot to collect some of them in the Spring. New beech saplings sprouted from the undergrowth and grew. Towering trees arranged by a forgetful Jay. The saplings were fueled by the Blue's droppings accumulating below. Moths transmuted into trees. And then the moths found the saplings and laid their eggs. And the caterpillars ate of the beech leaf. Tree transmuted into moth again. And the Blue landed on the sapling and found her quarry, the moth. And so it went.

4

RAIN AND GRUBS

rip. drip. drip. Glistening droplets grew and fell, grew and fell, one after another; careening down the carpet surface of damp green mosses. They fell further, tracing invisible grooves onto a smoothed rockface. Finally, imperceptibly adding to the growing, trickling procession: its route preordained by a shifting forest.

The Eft watched the processions of the microscopic world intently. The bead of water bending and stretching where the forces of adhesion and cohesion birthed a living amoeba. The Eft saw the translucent, watery mass crawl along endlessly: this mimic of life and source of life, all in one. Only the Eft was close enough to hear the gentle drip, to watch the amoebic flow down the mosses. The Eft continued on, dutifully following the path of least resistance. It crawled a long, circuitous path around the boulder. Sliding its slick belly along the rotting mulch of leaf litter, unbothered by the impervious, towering behemoth that made its years-long journey subtly longer. A learnèd patience. The Eft knew—as water did—that in time, any path could be forged.

Beyond that micro-environment, the drumming beat of the heavy La Niña downpour drowned all sound, and more than a few small creatures. Heavy drops fell, bounding off the waxy leaves and exploding against unmoving branches and boulders. The deafening white noise stretched out, overwhelming all else. The rain was so heavy there was no hiding from it. And though the downpour meant bounty and plenty, that did nothing to dry sopping wet feathers from which glistening drops grew and fell, grew and fell. Manna from heaven that you couldn't escape.

It rained all night. The Blue sat puffed out with wet body feathers erect in every direction, her body fighting to hold warmth in a shrinking temperature gradient. Nine grams of defiance against the onslaught of the entire outside world. She was down at the base of the beech tree, holed up underneath a hobble leaf. She persisted somewhere between soaked and moist. Once through the night the leaf gathered a modest puddle, it overcame the strength of the plant's own trapped vascular waters and dipped the entire accumulated sip onto her head. Just as she was reaching a warm-ish equilibrium.

She kept her head half bowed; her eyes half-closed in stressed concentration—that universal, secular prayer. Unlike the tedium of migration, the long hours of rain held fast the entirety of her attention. She could scarcely hold a single thought outside of the all-encompassing discomfort. Her mind raced in a pointless cycle; retreading a hopeless fantasy of escape from her situation. The faculties reserved for survival set to wasteful spiraling, raging against the inevitable. Her body took away the executive reigns only to ponder basest existence.

She would survive. She knew the limits of her own body, the rigors she could withstand. The inescapable discomfort—barely lessened in intensity by her found bastion of hobble—is one familiar to all creatures. Abject comfort on demand is not a common experience anywhere, least of all in the Abenaki Hills. One weathers it as surely as one jaunts through the sun-washed joy of a sunny morning. These moments make up what it means to be alive. And neither the ups nor the downs last for long. All must be endured. Tomorrow would come when it was ready.

~

DEW GLOWED in the morning light, illuminating the glistening forest still wet from that night. Life was back to its busy cycles. The Blue hung precariously upside down under a hobble leaf three times her size. A miniature spider crawled along the underside wearily. It was not committing any harrowing feat: at this miniscule size, gravity meant little and the sticky forces that clung it to the leaf made up its entire world. The Blue who watched it intently was herself on the razor's edge between these worlds. Ingenious avian engineering made her just light enough to remain unburdened by gravity and employ it as a tool if she so wished. She lunged, and *crunch!* The arachnid

was no more. She made a rapid survey of her surroundings before swallowing and leaping to the
next leaf.

Again, she hung upside down, suspended centimeters above the ground. She could hear a hefty
caterpillar, but the leaf was empty. She looked
around, at leaves to her right and to her left. Then
she craned her neck back, back, till her forehead
pressed against her rump (a feat reserved only for
birds) and she saw it. It was right beneath her.
Juicy and slow and oblivious, a chunky larvae
wriggling on the forest floor. Not one of the toxic
spine-laden larvae either. This Luna Moth larvae
invested its entire evolutionary risk aversion in its
vibrant green coat. It was designed to blend in
with the endless forest. But a centimeter away
from its predator, crawling slowly across
browning leaf litter, it shone like a welcome bea-
con. She hesitated for a fraction of a second. It
was perhaps too much for her by herself, much
more suited to feeding a new brood. But that
wouldn't stop her from partaking. She wouldn't
have to hunt again till evening—

Fwooop! Some unseen blur stole the larva out
from under her. One moment it was there and the
next it was gone; only turbid leaf refuse settling
back down remained. She dropped down to
where her prey had been and looked about fever-
ishly. Now was no time to pout if there was some
capable predator nearby—

It was a male. A Black-Throated Blue Warbler
male. Not the rude male from the day before, but
a new, less impressive specimen—holding her
grub! She chirped. The male spun around and

looked at her curiously. He probably hadn't seen her hanging above. She had failed to notice him, after all. They were both so focused on that obvious treat. *If only I hadn't hesitated.*

"Hey! Hey you!" she spouted.

The male turned and hopped a few hops away. *The indignant creature!* She lunged after him. She was tired of being treated so poorly. That was *her* grub. As far as she could tell this wasn't even the male's territory. It was neutral ground! No man's land! (Ignoring the countless intersecting and invisible enclaves of other species) The male looked back long enough to realize he was being pursued. He likely surmised that she was after the grub. He hopped with renewed vigor. He couldn't fly with such a heavy prize; all he could manage was a fluttering hop. She landed in front of him, fuming. But he spun around, kicked off the root of the tree and hopped the other way. She followed, her chest pounding and her little heart fluttering at a rate that would kill larger animals. The male cut in close to the tree to gain ground, together they had circled clear to the other side.

He narrowly misjudged his direction and found himself face to face with a root, one too tall to clear while keeping the whole grub with him. Again, she fluttered past him and landed atop the root. She had him now, there was nowhere he could escape to. She hopped down and approached. The male looked everywhere. She leapt for the grub—still alive and wiggling in primitive terror—but he slighted back, his agility matching her own. This male might be dull both in color and strategy, but he was quick.

She reassessed the situation. She saw that she had managed to pierce the grub on one side. Green goop beaded from its wound. Her mouth watered.

For a moment they circled each other. She knew the male couldn't outrun her with the heavy loot, and he must know it too. But it was not unheard of for males to fight a female. Still, she couldn't know what he would do. She steeled herself and tried to appear outwardly nonchalant, unpredictable enough to not betray her intentions. She gave him the slip—diving again! But something stopped her short. The male leapt back—and found himself in a pool of morning light rays. The light glinted off the dew and caught something at his feet. A metal band! And another, a colored band of bright green plastic. Both familiarly gripping his ankles. She couldn't believe what she was seeing. She was dumbfounded. The male watched her warily, head cocked.

Her mind raced. Was this a sign? Was he another chosen? When did he get them, as a nestling or an adult? Did he know any more than her what the trinkets meant? Her interest in the helpless larva evaporated and her pupils dilated in intense focus. This time she wouldn't let him get away, she had to learn everything he knew!

"You—you have the trinkets?" she blurted. She immediately regretted her tactless outburst. Embarrassed, she waited for a response. The male was quiet.

"On your legs, like mine, see?" She motioned with one leg, jangling them and catching the light. The male dropped the grub and hopped over to her, closing the distance between them. For a moment an awkward standstill bewitched the odd pair. The male watched her intently. Not her legs, not her trinkets, but her.

She started again, "Whe—When did you get yours? As a nestling?"

His entire stance had changed, his focus shifted. His eyes dilated as well. Was it—mutual understanding? The male roused, expanding all his feathers to reset them from the chaos of the chase. Then without any sort of lead up, the male began a display dance. He bounded from side to side and sang—

Zoooo zoooo zweeee! Zoo zweeee! Zoo zweeee!

She was jarred out of her trance for a moment and utterly confused. First the grub, then the trinkets, and now this! The male had gone from competitor to suitor with scarcely an intervening thought. He took up his dance again with renewed vigor, determined to push through her apparent disinterest. He fluttered up to a low bush, and alighted on a branch plucked bare by sawflies. The grub lay unclaimed on the forest floor below. The male threw out his wings and pulled them back in. Out and in. Out and in. He sang again and presented his flank. Then he dove back down and landed right in front of her. Hopping left and right, forward and back. He flattened out showing his flank. Pause. Opposite flank. Pause. Then back up to the branch. His chest heaved as he fought to keep up his pace and volume. He sang again insistently.

She was not caught breathless by his dulled colors and ratty tail feathers. Not like the other male. But she was transfixed by his trinkets. And she was admittedly impressed by his performance if still a bit dazed at the emotional roller coaster of the last few moments. It was clear to her now that the male had mistook her hesitation for sudden attraction. At the very end of their pursuit, at that crucial moment when she had had him, she conspicuously hesitated. A helpful misconstrue that had caused him to reconsider the value of the grub, versus the value of taking this opportunity to impress her. Of course, in some ways he had been right. She had the opportunity to steal the grub and get a head start when he leapt to the bare bush to sing his heart out. But instead, she had waited to see the rest of his display.

Another thought crept into her mind. With his agility and determination, a male like this would be a resourceful hunter. A capable provider. She deigned to watch him dance a bit longer.

Finally, visibly exhausted he landed. Delicately he picked up the contested grub (still writhing in pain), and presented it at her feet. A fitting gift to outstrip an already impressive performance. If she took the grub now, it would be assenting to his advances. Well played.

She bit into the juicy grub and savored it. She would mate with this curious male and together they would learn the secrets of their trinkets.

5

NESTING

And so the two were paired. For weeks they moved together as a single unit. Their former chase turned to a ruthless, coordinated pack-hunt. No grub stood a chance. There was more than enough to eat. They both ate well and commanded a wide, rich territory. A territory defined by the tortured sugar maple at its center; its form twisted into position by patient indigenous peoples centuries prior. All around the maple was an unbroken sea of thick hobble. Beyond that was the unruly forest. A veritable wall of birch widely encircled the sugar maple like some impenetrable enclave. Their own private sanctum away from the world.

After a long evening of patrolling their territory, singing occasionally to proclaim sovereignty, they would retire to the pinnacle of that tall, twisted maple and mate. A concise act in the world of Warblers, precluded by gentle foreplay of dancing and playful chase. They would mate three, sometimes four times a day, often following feeding. The male would sing for her still, but without all the gaudy, energy-sapping intensity of that first display dance. Now it was a reaffirmation of their dedication to each other. A quiet song for the female and for the nest. Simple and private. Then, they would dive together down towards the forest floor picking up where they left off; their ceaseless deadly hunt.

Gradually, their mental programming drove them to the art of nest-making. They scoured the forest for small sticks and dried leaf fragments. The male discovered where a large, branching stick had fallen amidst the hobble, suspended by the viney mats. This would become the base of their nest. The female wrested spider's silk from an orb weaver (a snack) and bound the dry beech leaves into an even mat over the stick framework. Together they surrounded and compacted this scaffolding with layers and layers of smaller sticks. Each the right curvature and length, like masonry, fitted perfectly into every opening to form an even, outer shell. The entire thing could fit into a cupped human hand. It hung suspended barely half a meter off the ground, intricately crafted. It was plump, fresh, and beautiful. All Blues hid their nests low like this. Comfortably set and camouflaged amidst the wood ferns and the hobble.

In the gloam of one misty eve, the female sat in her fresh new nest. So small was the nest that her tail stuck out one end, and her head jutted out the other. Her body tensed and shuddered. It was clear she was in some sort of pain, but it did not

make it to her eyes. She waited stoically until *plop!*
Something round and slick rolled and settled into
the bottom of the nest: an egg. She hopped up
from her awkward post and stood on the edge,
inspecting the thing curiously. It was tan colored,
slightly oblong, and speckled with a smattering of
brown spots. It was still shiny and wet. Her dis-
torted mirror-image looked up at her, fisheye and
cast in ghostly tan-brown form. The first of four
she would lay over the next four days, one egg
a day.

Last year she didn't understand what was happening. Her first egg had not even made it to the
nest but instead was carelessly laid on the ground
and tumbled down a hill. (Blues of course have no
way of transporting an egg to its proper place
once laid.) The other three were laid in their
shoddy nest of last year, and even hatched. But
mere days after her wriggling, naked pink offspring had emerged, Blue Jays had chased her and
her mate off the nest and taken them all. That
year she had started a second nest, but malnutri-
tion meant her body refused to produce another
brood before migration took her back out to the
Caribbean.

Now she looked down at this first egg with a
knowing resolve. Her progeny, her bloodline, the
most important thing in the known universe. This
year *would* be different. She knew what she was
doing.

Just then a loud *JEER! JEEEER!* rang out
through the trees. It was answered by a racket; the
snapping of beaks and hammering of bills. A loud
flapping of many wings somewhere far above.

The Blue hopped back onto her nest, instinctively covering her shiny, round progeny. She couldn't see where in the growing dark, but somewhere there was a family of Blue Jays passing by. Their eyes were similarly unsuited to the night, and it was unlikely they had seen her. They were probably just heading to roost.

They were never far. The enemy.

A Blue Jay can weigh up to a hundred grams. More than ten times the weight of a Blue. And five times their length. Unlike the Warblers, these masters of intelligence traveled in large family groups of five to ten individuals. A great chaotic mass, hunting and scavenging together. Parents and progeny learning from each other. These fearsome creatures would happily pluck the hairs off deer and dogs alike if they wanted it for their nests. Promptly taking flight before the large mammals could respond properly to the nuisance. Jays would steal kibble from domestic pets when they fancied it. They would fight off foxes for the remains of roasted chicken carcass tossed by dumpsters. And unlike Warblers, these formidable Jays would often visit the strange human bird feeders. If too many Finches and Sparrows were present, the Jays would mimic the calls of hawks from a distance to chase the others off. Any who were brave enough to stay would be harassed and attacked by the Blue Jay posse. They were unstoppable.

They were creatures between two worlds. The Weaver Finches stuck to human settlements and the Warblers stuck to the forests, but the Jays moved freely between the two. Masters of both worlds. In the forests when they weren't collecting tree nuts or hunting small insects, they were seeking out and devouring the nestlings of other birds with impunity. Their cackling cries rang out through the trees. All others fled under their shadow. Only the Hawks and Eagles—whose calls they mimic'd—stood higher on the food chain. This land was theirs and they knew it. The Blue, for her part, knew she would have to use every trick she had learned to keep those monsters at bay. And even then, it might not be enough.

THE NEXT WEEK went by uneventfully. The other three eggs came dutifully and without incident. In a stroke of luck, the fast-growing woodferns unrolled above and around their nest, further obscuring it. The male continued to find hearty game and so far, they faced no territorial contest. His feathers even took on a bit more shine than when they had met. Their combined efforts yielded a healthy and consistent bounty for the pair benefitting them both greatly. But now the female spent most of her days sitting on the nest. Her head jutting out at a 45-degree angle at one end, her tail sticking out at a similar angle opposite, forever shrouded in the fractal shade of the woodferns. She kept a wary eye on the distant canopy above but overall sat contented for many hours. Her nest was adequately shielded, and it stayed cool through high noon and reasonably dry through the rain.

She hopped out of her nest only to relieve herself and to take a sip of dew accumulated on the ferns around her. The male arrived like clockwork now, every fifteen to twenty minutes to deliver some morsel or to check on her before returning to his watch. He fed her like a chick, carrying some many-legged arthropod to her while she sat. She herself would leave the nest only once a day, for perhaps thirty minutes maximum to supplement her feeding and stretch her aching legs. Otherwise, they were both consumed by their duties. Her only visible landmark was the sugar maple. The trunk took an unnatural right angle, running parallel to the forest floor a good meter and a half before continuing skyward just as abruptly. It was a strange but comfortable home.

You would think the many hours ticking by would lead to impossible boredom. But unlike the Jays or the humans, the Blue was not burdened by so vast a mind that it had to be occupied at every waking moment. The simple knowledge that she was fulfilling her greatest purpose was more than enough to satiate her idle thoughts. Contentedness let her rest easy and watch the gentle swaying of the leaves in the midday breeze. Though sometimes—quietly to herself, so quiet her eggs could scarcely hear—she would whistle tunelessly to herself. The female song (and yes, females do have a song) was not as rigid or structured as the male's. It flowed freely hither and thither, governed only by the unknowable inclinations of her subconscious. Sometimes her song took on a familiar jangle. An echo of the remembered sound of her 'trinkets' clattering in the wind. A subconscious reminder of that closely held secret. Her instincts had all but forced it from her mind these past few weeks but some inkling of it was still there. And so it was that she passed many hours with her meandering song. Her smooth turquoise wards were warm and reassuring against her bare belly. At least for today, all was right in the world.

6

NOEPE'S WINTER

The male had spent the winter on the island of Noepe. The ocean-regulated temperatures kept everything above freezing, and there were enough morsels to feed a modest population of overwintering Warblers. At least it was enough for the clever Warblers.

He had dug around in the cavities of rotting, fallen trees. There, wedged deep in the grain he found crickets and grasshoppers that had let themselves willingly freeze over. It was a unique survival strategy they employed, an arthropodan hibernation. Often their solitary pocket was protected by freshly packed sawdust. Like a healed wound, the packed sawdust was never quite flush and always had the quality of scar tissue in the soft wood. The Blue learned to spot these freshly corked sanctuaries by the subtle differences in wood grain. If you could get past the icy crunch, each arthropod popsicle promised a nutrient-rich morsel that wouldn't bite, run, or musk you. The male ate well with little competition.

Unlike most other Blues, he loved to be social. Even in the off season. Without many other Warblers to spend the short winter days with, he found himself immersed in a Chickadee flock. It had actually been purely by accident.

One day like any other, his foraging took him into the exact range and coincidental timing of a large, nomadic mixed flock. One moment he was counting his good luck at his bounty (by pecking at his own trinkets—a superstitious tick he'd developed), and the next a veritable swarm had accosted the bushes around him. A cacophony of cheeps and chirps engulfed the woods. The male was in shock. The visitors mostly ignored him. After only a few moments they all flushed up into the high branches and disappeared. He could hear the flurry of calls carrying down the far hill. It was as if a gust had carried them away all at once.

After a quick preening to collect himself, he returned to his forage and still managed to find enough arthropodsicles to make lunch. The whole rest of the day he couldn't stop himself from looking after the direction that the flock had fled. He made up his mind to visit this same spot again tomorrow.

The spot in question was a low, flat depression in the otherwise hilly terrain, covered evenly with loose pine needles. There was very little ground cover, the needles seemed to suffocate anything green, and in the chilly winter months doubly so. A spacious woodland surrounded the depression. The entire area was on a gentle incline which gave all the trees a slight lean uphill from a foraging bird's low-ground vantage. A winding, man-made gravel trail snaked through the pines heading towards a scenic overlook at the cliff-face a hundred meters passed. Even from here you could hear the unforgiving crash of the waves of the north side of the island. The perpetual salt spray kept the whole area mildly humid and the soil salt-hardened. But the slight depression gave enough of a reprieve from the elements, the wind and the spray and foot-path visitors, that it had a higher-than-usual accumulation of arthropodsicles, berry bushes and grass seeds for the prospective forager. On the scale of a Warbler, it was practically a lush mountain valley.

For the next three days he visited and foraged. For those next three days, the flock blew through like a hurricane right around lunch. On the third day, some members recognized and acknowledged him. A Bohemian Waxwing: a striking bird, silky reddish-brown all over with red-and-yellow tipped wings and tail, an impressive crest, and black mask around its eyes—alighted down from the rest to alert the Blue to an arthropodsicle he had missed. This one must have been watching his technique. The Blue used his specialized, insect-eating beak to extract the treat and shared it with the Waxwing (whose own beak was optimized for berries).

Later in the day, a Chickadee: a black-and-white bird with a black cap and bib, white cheeks and gray back, an extra-large head and fierce demeanor—rushed past the Blue to chase off a

Kestrel that had perched above. It bravely called *DEEE-DEEE-DEEE-DEEE-DEEE* before plucking a single head-feather from the poor Kestrel. The small bird of prey—who hadn't been doing anything in particular yet—got the message. The Kestrel gave a protesting call before flying off to another branch a few trees away.

The Blue was awestruck at the show of valor. As far as he was concerned, that Chickadee had just saved his life. The gallant defender flew back down and gave an inquisitive trill with the equivalent of cocking its head to one side (rotating its face a full 90 degrees so it was now looking *up* at the warbler). The Blue understood. He hopped forward and answered the trill. The Chickadee flew up to a high branch of a gnarled hickory and looked back. The Blue followed. Below them, a White-Breasted Nuthatch, a tiny teardrop shaped bird with a pastel-blue mantle and white belly, paused his probing search under the bark with his boat-shaped bill and looked up expectantly. The Chickadee cried out *DEEE-DEEE*—and the entire flock took to the air. The Blue followed at their tail. Just like that, he had joined the flock.

Such flocks were not strangers to, well, strangers. The Chickadees were well known for leading bands of Nuthatches, Kinglets, Waxwings, and Warblers on their ceaseless foraging trek circling Noepe. It was an arrangement common throughout the country. Foraging flocks like these could be found from coast to coast. They were always led by Chickadees; Carolina Chickadees in the east and south; Black Capped Chickadees in the west; Boreal Chickadees up north. The fearless Chickadee would keep an eye out and call out any threats. If an Owl or Hawk came too close, the band of Chickadees would fight it. Even a predator a hundred times their size would not be spared their animus. The Blue was deeply impressed. Though he'd never chased an owl alongside them, watching that blur of black and white, he thought he could someday, maybe.

CHICKA-DEEE-DEEE-DEEE-DEEE. The bubbly, nasally call that was their namesake. Four or five *dee*'s constituted a serious threat like a Hawk or a domestic cat. Three *dee*'s an annoyance like a Blue Jay or Redwing Blackbird. One or two *dee*'s was a non-threat like a lumbering old dog or a human. In return, the various members of their flock would employ their specialties to pilfer an eclectic buffet for all. The Nuthatch found concealed bugs hidden under the loose bark of trees. The Waxwing plucked berries from bushes. The Kinglets and occasional Flycatcher nabbed flying insects from the air. And the Warblers plucked arthropods of all sorts from underneath leaves and flowers.

Occasionally others in the flock would break from foraging to peck at his trinkets, 'charms' he called them in his own mind. Good luck charms. He didn't mind the pecking; they would peck, and he would take comfort in the idea that he had given his fellows some good luck. It was a sentiment he had held from an early age; from his first autumn back in the Abenaki Hills. Where they had first provided comfort and hope when everything was going wrong.

. . .

As THE ONLY male and the runt of his brood, his three sisters picked on him often. They wouldn't let him forget about his 'charms', pecking at them incessantly. He pecked at them too, desperate to get them off his ankles in the beginning. Eventually he gave up, but his sisters never did.

"You're not my brother. You're a monster who's replaced him. Sent to torment us!" his eldest sister would say. She would spend hours taunting him, pecking at him. His other two sisters kept to themselves, avoiding him like he carried sickness.

He would seek refuge closer to the nest where his mother readily fed him. While the others were starting to forage for themselves, he, the runt, found comfort in the closeness. His mother wasn't bothered by his 'charms'. Nor did she think he was a monster. She told him she had seen when he got them. Her retellings captured him in rapt attention.

His sisters had bounded out of the nest. Still flightless they plopped onto the leaf litter below and waddled away. But he, still flightless and blind, had stayed. His mother continued her warning alarm, but he was too undeveloped to get out of the nest in time. She watched helplessly as those odd, looming behemoths plucked him from her nest.

"They looked like humans, but I couldn't be sure. I had only heard about humans from the gossip of Starlings, never seen one myself." She told him. It was her first year nesting; she had fledged the previous year and spent her own winter on Noepe. His mother's autumn and now summer was spent deep in the woods. She couldn't be sure because her neck of the woods had been void of human contact, even during migration. But that was her guess. And because humans were like crows, 'doing strange things for no reason', she had told him. Even then he had had a hard time accepting her explanation.

"The ways of humans are unknowable," his mother had retorted. And that was the end of the conversation. This was years before the other female Blue would receive her own 'trinkets' and suffer interrogation in the migratory flock from the Caribbean. There was no one for him to compare with; no one else that shared in his strange fate. At least none near their territory.

Days later the Blue Jays—overall blue-colored with a white belly; black-barred wings accented by a bold white wingbar; with a prominent head crest; and a bold, black necklace—came for them. He and his sisters were spread out over maybe the ten square meters of forest surrounding their nest site. Although they were 'foraging' none of them were very good at it. All of the siblings were still getting help from their mother to meet the demands of their rapidly growing bodies and sprouting juvenile plumage. Their father had already headed east for migration. Not because he was a bad father, but because that was the way of their species, as it had been since time immemorial. First the males left for migration, then the females, and finally the juveniles. Distantly he heard his mother's alarm calls. Although he didn't yet see the attackers, he instinctively dropped to the forest floor, shielded by layers of hobble and fern. He was not yet flighted, but managed to break his fall a little (being an eight-gram fledgling meant plummeting to the ground wasn't a big deal). There among the leaf litter he found his oldest sister.

She hissed quietly, "you've brought the monsters to us, evil little brother."

He ignored her and held his breath. Just above, the hulking shadow of an adult Blue Jay choked out the evening light shimmering through the leaves. Its head darted about; its crest bobbed erratically. The Jay communicated with the others in its family group in piercing, fitful bursts. There was no way to tell what it was saying. That impenetrably complex language of Jays and other corvids evaded the minds of the little songbirds. It could not be outsmarted, outpaced, or bested. Their only hope was to keep quiet and lay low.

It was at that moment that the polished silvery metal of his 'charm' glinted in the evening light. The angle was just right and the sunlight refracted, casting a glowing square against a nearby fallen branch. The Blue's fearful crouch and subtle lean of his ankle made the square move along the branch. The glow shimmied up and up, unnaturally wrinkling against the rough surface of the trunk. Neither Warbler noticed it at first, but the Jay certainly did. It spun around and its crest shot straight up. It watched the square's lifelike movement, accented by the gentle sway of the wind. Its eyes dilated in intense fascination. By now both Blues below had seized on the source of distraction of their pursuer. They too watched the glowing square of light from their vantage and were as confused as the Jay, though they remained frozen in place—*JEEEER!*, the Jay called to the others.

The Jay looked back down and refocused on the pair. There was no point in running. They couldn't fly. The poor fledglings hardly had the instinct to flee, so they stared dumbly upward at this death-incarnate. Its deep black eyes shimmering. It clacked its sharp beak and hopped over, its head held stone-still in space, its body orienting around it, a testament to its singular, deadly fixation.

"I hope it eats you first," his sweet sister said under her breath. He turned to respond, but before he could think of any witty last words, the glowing square of light rushed ahead of them bounding impossibly fast over branches, leaves, and trees. It was unimpeded by the physical limitations of the thick forest. Even the Blues watched after its breathless path in hushed awe.

The Blue Jay watched it too. It was perhaps the one thing that could pull its attention from the slow-moving, easy meals below. It was something both novel and shiny. With one last look to the pair, the would-be devourer of fledglings bounded away. One hop, two hops, then it took flight and disappeared. The wind from its powerful wingbeat pressed on both Blue siblings hard enough that they crumpled. They were both speechless. The male would see the strange glowing square 'bug' only a handful of times again in its life but would never guess at its secret.

Later, the two siblings stayed close and investigated through the forest. Neither sibling looked like their parents yet, but they were acting more like adults every day. All over their bodies sprouted fresh juvenile feathers. The new feathers were drab and itched like hell. They projected out from blood-filled shafts in clumped rows. They tested out their nimble, newly feathered bodies and found they could manage something of an 'extended hop' on their stubby primary feathers. There was comparatively little danger now, the Jays had since left for the season and the two were flighted enough to avoid the occasional threat from below. It took them several days to survey the entire territory. Hopping together, they checked their nest, the trees their mother had fed them on, even the farthest borders of their father's territory. Despite their long search, they never found their mother or two sisters. Evidently the Jays had gotten them all.

After giving up the search they continued to work as a flock of two: foraging and traveling and learning their new bodies. Nearly all of the adults had migrated by then, and the forest was littered with awkward juveniles. It was a confusing time but a relatively peaceful one. And though it took them many long hours to forage in their inexperienced state, the two managed to stave off hunger. His sister never fully grew to trust him, but the Blue remembered his time with his sister fondly.

Their long warm days gave way to the subtle chill and early nights of the encroaching fall. After another couple of days, they separated and migrated; their tenuous dedications to each other lost in the necessities of migration and the alienation of male and female. The next year when all the Blues returned to the forest, he briefly spied his older sister. She saw him too, but didn't acknowledge him. And as quickly as he saw her, she disappeared into the brush with a male, her mate he guessed. He hadn't seen his older sister since. Perhaps she died. Or maybe she took up a territory far away from him and their paths never crossed. In all likelihood she never thought of him.

YEARS PASSED. The little male had his own mate and their own brood. Their first season they struggled. Their nest was partially predated while both were briefly away. Before they could begin to mourn a terrible storm and flood had carried off the remainder. It was still early in the season, so they tried again. (Rearing a second brood was not uncommon) The second brood fared better, but again partial predation took all but one of the nestlings. That nestling fledged under their extra-vigilant watch. But neither of them ever saw it again after they left for migration. Fledglings were easy pickings after the parents left, they could never be sure what happened to it.

The seasons continued their ceaseless march forward. In the blink of a nictitating membrane, the next season was upon them. The male found his mate from the previous year, and they were paired again. She had a new injury along her flank and didn't want to talk about it. They had a successful brood. Through a little bit of luck and a half dozen 'injured wing' displays, they managed to avoid all predators and reared four healthy fledglings. Again they tried for a second brood and for a while it held, but a freak cold snap sapped away much of the steady stream of arthropods and they starved. The two parents, themselves malnourished, watched helplessly as their babies withered away and one by one died in the nest. It was horrible, and it took all the joy from their early season success. They abandoned the nest and did not try again. In fact they didn't spend much time together, opting to forage in solitary reflection till the real cold of winter sent them south again.

The next season came and the male dutifully arrived at their same spot, determined to do even better this year. The female was not there. He waited one day, then two, then a week. She never showed up and he never saw her again. He sang for a time, but his heart wasn't in it.

A curious feature of Black Throated Blue society is that they will sometimes engage in 'extra pair copulations'. Paired females will find males in other territories (often themselves paired for the season) and discreetly mate with them. Such salacious rendezvous offered two things; a wider genetic pool to increase the chances of healthy offspring, and males that will go out of their way to feed the nestlings of other nests on the off chance that one or two might be their offspring. After two 'extra pair copulations', the male stopped singing and spent the season alone. He foraged by himself, chatted with the occasional Warbler or Wood Creeper he encountered and lived a bachelor's life. He was utterly miserable.

The next season he met a new mate who was full of energy. They had a flourishing, life-filled season and reared three successful broods together. All twelve nestlings fledged and both parents ran themselves absolutely ragged. He promised himself he would never do that again, in spite of the pride he and his mate felt at their success. Just before the end of the season, some mammal got hold of his mate and she was gone. He migrated alone then, the emotional stress of the full life of a warbler taxing his limited capacities. After a season like that he was happy to get back to Noepe.

IT HAD BEEN a long time in Warbler years. Today, he was twice the age his mother had ever been. He had catalogued a lot of life lessons, suffered tragedy and great success. He thought again about his charms. He had seen humans up close, but had a hard time believing they were attaching charms to nestlings. They almost never ventured this deep in the woods. And what was the point? All he knew was that he and his sister were the only survivors of the Jay attack. He who had incessantly pecked at his charms. And she who had mercilessly bullied him, pecking at the charms nearly as often. Somehow, some way, the charms had saved them from the Jays. He had no idea how, but he knew.

Now he pecked them all the time. Not a flustered, desperate pecking to remove them. And not in the antagonistic, tormenting way his sister had pecked them. But like counting rosary beads—

absently comforting himself in times of strife. He learned on his first migration that others were prone to peck at them as well. Out of curiosity or annoyance or feeding instinct; it didn't matter what drew them. There was something intimately universal to him about others seeking that blessing of luck that had kept him safe all these years.

And so, in this new foraging flock of every shape and color—led by the dauntless Chickadees–the Blue discovered some nostalgia of home. Of safety. For two years he flew with the Noepe flock and fared well in spite of the scarcities of winter. Being this far north carved out a special niche for those willing to brave it, and like his mother before him he found his own way. He paid especially close attention to the Chickadee leaders of the flock, studying their tendencies. He watched and practiced their agile moves. He resolved to carry their fearlessness in his own tiny heart wherever he went. He would never shy away from the looming shadow of the Blue Jay again.

The stresses of the cold meant his breeding plumage was never as glossy or vibrant as he would have liked. It bothered him but he never thought to discard his routine or his winter flock for any promise of warmer waters. He was, after all, old for a Blue. Entering his fifth season now in Abenaki. (Birds didn't show age in the way mammals did, and it didn't translate to any 'age gap' between him and his new mate) He had fathered more than eight broods now. Some had failed, some had fledged. Every fledgling could in theory rear its own brood the very next season. By now, his genetic lineage had grown larger than he could ever fathom. Despite his age, he was as quick as any Chickadee. He was quite good at being a Black-Throated Blue Warbler, charms or not.

7

THE JAYS

Four floundering, wriggling blobs huddled together. Their pinkish skin was wrinkly and semi-transparent. As delicate as rice paper. Their eyes were tightly shut and would be for several more days. Four oversized bobble-heads teetered precariously on impossibly skinny necks, begging skyward. Their yellow beaks were agape. Each nestling barely weighed six grams and looked as if they could fall apart at any moment. They were her perfect babies.

Both adults were off the nest regularly now. Foraging constantly to satisfy the endless hunger of four new mouths. (To say nothing of their own growing hunger) They rarely spoke during these hectic days. They rarely saw each other except in high-speed passing. One parent ferrying a grub towards the nest, the other leaving to find more. Back and forth they dashed through all waking hours of the day. It went by like a blur. They knew only exhaustion and speed. This new rhythm of their lives was the quintessential challenge new parents of most species find.

Their efforts paid off. All four grew quickly and were healthy. Five days in, the begging had not ceased, but there were no runts in this nest. All four of the plump little creatures threatened to spill out of the edges of the tiny nest. They were nearly as large as adults now, but they were still featherless, pink, and wrinkly. One morning—like magic—all four had their eyes open. (Though when one peered deep into those eyes, one could scarcely detect a single thought behind them) They had even started squeaking—some semblance of an unpracticed Blue chirp.

JEEEER JEEEEEEEER. The Blue looked up at them, six Jays in total. She watched from the safety of the nest, having just forced a rather large grub down the throat of one of her babies. They alighted on a high branch of the Sugar Maple and surveyed the thick, summer forest. So many heads, like a Lernaean Hydra, looking in every direction at once.

One Jay with an all-white head (*Leucism* or a partial loss of pigment wasn't uncommon in birds, but it was striking in this Jay) dove, plummeting like a rock. At the last moment its wings flew out and it landed atop the hobble thicket. It hopped along a few branches and then–*nab!* it grabbed an unsuspecting orb weaver. The Jay family group was out foraging.

A more delicate fluttering filled the air, the Blue recognized it immediately. The flutter of a Warbler's wings. It was her mate. From her vantage she saw him enter the clearing and immediately veer off, making a hard U-turn and disappearing again from view. Clearly he had spotted the Jays. It was a close call, but the Jays weren't there looking for any Blue nestlings. Not yet. As long as he didn't fly to the nest, they wouldn't find it. She hoped they hadn't seen her fly in. *They couldn't have or they would have been on top of me already*, she told herself. If they stayed quiet and didn't move, the Jay family would get their fill of spiders and grubs and move on.

She couldn't see the male but most likely he was waiting on some high branch until the Jays left. Their territory was so productive that there was plenty to go around. Although Jays could be cruel, it was just so much easier to forage for themselves. There was still a chance they'd chase him for his grub, but it was slim. Funnily enough it was probably the Jays' 'territory' as well, although in her tense state, this idea didn't occur to her. She held her breath and told herself they were safe; they wouldn't find the nest. They hadn't so far, even after all this time.

She could hear the white-headed Jay coming closer, its immense size clattering through the dense underbrush. She held her breath. *Cheep cheep cheeeep!* She spun around. One of her babies chirped its little begging call. It was the one she just fed. It had managed to swallow the large grub and was of course hungry for more. The nestlings had associated the presence of an adult with the arrival of food. After a moment, the other three chimed in, *cheep cheep cheeep!* The fact that their mother had not left since their most recent feeding was totally lost on the small creatures. Ever the bottomless stomachs. She had stayed perched on the edge of the nest far too long. But leaving would put a clear target on the nest. She had no way to tell them to shut up. She couldn't communicate what danger they were in. She looked to and fro, unsure what to do.

The clatter in the underbrush stopped, and the ominous silence that ensued conveyed a sense that something somewhere was listening intently. The noisy progression had at least somewhat covered the insistent calls of her nestlings, but now it was obvious Whitehead had heard them. She could just make out its bright, white head through the thick vines and ferns. It was looking right at her. Silently stalking her now.

JEEEEEER JEEEEEEER! Whitehead's crest shot straight up and it called to its siblings.

JEEEER! High above the others peered downward through curious eyes. They didn't see Whitehead's quarry, but they knew he stalked some prize in the hobble below. The other Jays continued looking down into the thicket trying to make out their prey.

Whitehead returned to its stalking. It was so close, it wasn't going to wait for its absent-minded siblings to descend down and steal this find. The Jay wasn't close enough to nab the adult Warbler it had spotted, but there was something else about this situation that pricked its intelligence. The Blue was just standing there, waiting. The Jay didn't know why just yet, but it resolved to figure it out.

Whitehead barreled forward, snapping twigs and parting leaves. A terrifying predatory display of single-minded determination. It made the Blue jerk from her otherwise stoic stance. Whitehead was the picture image of its ancient ancestral theropods pursuing their prey. Indeed, this was a story that had played out in various forms for millions of years, albeit at times on a much larger scale and in very different habitats.

High above, the male Blue had a clear view of what was happening. He dropped the grub he had been carrying, and at least one of the Jays dove for it. The other four Jays continued peering down at their sibling. Their wings twitched as they prepared to join Whitehead below. The Blue knew his mate would stand no chance if they all came down on the nest. He had to buy her time. The Chickadee in his heart compelled him forward.

He flew towards the Jays and gave a territory call. He hadn't given himself time to think through the consequences. And luckily so, or he might have been glued in place by the horror of facing four adult Blue Jays. The distance between the Blue and his colossal adversaries was so great there was no possibility of surprise. Nevertheless, he flew right at them. He was less than a second from meeting the four Jays face to face. At least two of the Jays stopped watching the forest floor to track the approach of this strange Warbler.

The male shut his eyes and pictured that fearless Chickadee. The one who attacked the Kestrel and saved his life. He mustered all his confidence. He turned and dove at the first Jay, deftly plucked a crest feather. He zoomed past them on his same course, clearing them before they could enact any immediate retaliation. It must have hurt because the Jay cried out. Good. The male spat out the large, blue crest-feather and turned around in time to see all four Jays had taken flight in pursuit!

Far below, the female watched Whitehead barrel ever closer, tracking the calls of her nestlings. It weaved between thick hobble stalks, kicking up leaf litter and small sticks. In a moment it would reach her. It became clear the Jay hadn't yet found a path to her. Its triangle-head darted about taking in the layers and layers of green.

She cursed herself for being born a species that these terrifying beasts found so delicious. She stole a precious second to look back down at her cheeping babies one last time. She didn't want to leave them here unprotected, but they wouldn't stop their begging.

She dove down to the ground and immediately the nestlings went silent. Then she hopped out in front of the Whitehead and made sure he was watching her. She stretched out one wing at a painful angle and hobbled away from it, but slowly. She made a pitiful, whining little chittering noise that sounded like a mix of pain and desperation. She had seen her mother do this once so long ago. Although she herself had never done it before, her performance now was perfect. The 'broken wing display' was genetically encoded into all Warblers as a failsafe to draw predators away from a nest or nestling.

It seemed to be working. Whitehead cocked its head sideways (his upturned crest jiggling with the intensity of his averted attention) and watched her. If she could hold its attention for long enough to draw it away from the nest, then maybe she could lose the Jay in the thicket. Of course, there was equal odds that it'd catch and kill her. Jays—and especially their family groups—were vicious hunters. They could easily take all of the Warblers in a fair fight.

High in the canopy, the male darted this way and that, narrowly avoiding the bites of the thick, clacking bills besieging him. He was bloodied, the Blue Jays in pursuit had nipped him twice on his rump. Even now they easily kept pace, threatening to overtake him. They were faster but he was more agile. If he could keep them on their wing tips—doubling back around trees and getting low—he might survive this encounter.

Like a gazelle fleeing a cheetah. A seal fleeing a killer whale. An old, old match up repeated endlessly throughout the animal kingdom. Predator and prey optimizing in opposite directions; determined to counter their opponent's advantage with their own.

OW! Another bite! One of the four had caught him on the ankle when he cut in tight around a large Birch. He could feel that they'd done some real damage this time. He tried to clench his foot. Sharp pain shot up his leg and told him that was a bad idea. He didn't know if he'd have use of his leg or indeed if it would ever heal. He couldn't think about it now. He could only do better on his next dodge. His mind raced; tracing the rush of branches before him, trying to pick the right moment.

A crooked branch stretched out with an inverted 'v' in its midsection gave him his opportunity. He feigned like he'd go over but narrowly, at the last possible moment he skimmed under the 'v'. He scraped some head feathers, but it was enough. The Jays went high. He dove low, surfing just above the layer of the hobble. For a second it felt like he'd completely evaded them. Then the other Jay hopped up from amidst the hobble right in front of him. It was the fifth Jay who had gone for his grub earlier. He veered right at the last second and flashed by the Jay at speeds that would have seriously injured them both if they'd collided. He'd outmaneuvered the murderous mob for at least a few seconds. Up ahead he saw his mate doing a broken wing display—was it a display? Or had the White-headed Jay got to her?

Discordant screeches above him told him he'd better keep moving. No time to get closer to help her. He spiraled upward in as tight a corkscrew as he could manage and cleared his five pursuers again. At the crest of his corkscrew, he stole a moment to look down at his nest. He knew exactly where it was buried in the hobble below. He wasn't worried about his pursuers following his sightline, it was too well hidden. He saw his four nestlings still there. Four little bobbleheads inquiring about absentmindedly, totally unaware of the battle raging beyond their safe walls of shredded bark fiber. Getting too high up was dangerous though, he went sideways. Without the cover of the thick forest, his speedy pursuers would surely catch him in the open air. Suddenly—

SQUEEEE SQUEEEEEEEE—

It was his mate, crying out—Whitehead had grabbed her by the 'injured' wing. She flapped wildly but couldn't break free. Her fake-timid cry broke out into a full scream of terror. So she had been faking, but wasn't fast enough to escape when Whitehead had decided to pounce.

He doubled back and past right through the middle of the Jay-flock behind him narrowly missing another bite. Then the Male tucked his wings and dove at terminal velocity. Whitehead spotted the tiny blue missile speeding towards it and deftly bounded out of the way. The male crashed into the ground and rolled. Weighing just shy of ten grams, it wasn't a fatal collision with the earth. It did hurt though. The little male spun onto his feet and assessed the situation before him. He had missed Whitehead, but the creature had let his mate free in its panicked evasion. The female darted by. For a split second, the two Black-Throated Blues looked into each other's eyes. They knew what the stakes were. They knew how hopeless it was. But both could see the shared resolve in the other's eyes. Wordlessly they knew. They would fight to the end, together. The female darted sideways, narrowly clearing the jaws of Whitehead and heading for the nest. The distant calls of the five other Jays echoed over their heads.

The male lunged forward, an ill-conceived frontal attack on a creature ten times his body weight. Whitehead bit at the male but grabbed only a mouthful of fright-molt; the loose body feathers unleashed to escape a predator. It was a trick that would work only once. The male arched upward above the Jay. His deeply injured foot burned with white-hot stabbing pain as he completed the maneuver. He knew under different circumstances he could dance circles around this lumbering beast, but his injuries and blood loss were slowing him down increasingly with every passing moment. He tried to push the pain into the back of his mind.

This time Whitehead thrust its wings out and rushed up to meet the hapless Blue. The male turned to meet the terrifying Jay below. The Male knew he wouldn't get another pass now that Whitehead was totally focused on him. He was going to make this count and pluck some head feathers, if he could just get lucky—

They met midair and Whitehead bit down hard before the male could maneuver. The Blue tensed for the killing blow, but it never came. He looked at where he'd been bitten. Whitehead had grabbed him by his charm! He had no time to lose. Stuck in the maw of the Jay and flapping wildly, he was perfectly positioned—*PECK!* He nabbed the Jay's eye clean from its socket. Whitehead pulled back in blinding shock and pain, minus one eye. The Jay's beak dropped little shattered flecks from where it had clamped down hard on the metallic band. The male Blue fell free, tumbling end over end. Both birds tumbled back to earth. Whitehead stumbled backwards, barely making it upright. It shook its head, once, twice, thrice, before realizing it could not clear its damaged vision. It looked down at the male with its remaining eye. An inquiring eye that looked deep within its Warbler opponent. The other eye still hanging from the little bird's jaw. For a moment the Jay was visibly confused. This Warbler was not a predator. At best it was a nuisance.

The Jay decided against any further engagement and took to the air, limping back to the higher branches on the Maple. There the creature settled, peering downward. Ignoring its own injuries for a moment to call out angrily to its siblings.

The female Blue made it back to the nest in what she hoped was just in time. Perhaps it didn't matter now. The others had found the nest. Five towering leviathan encircled the nest with its precious, squishy morsels within. She landed on the opposite rim and gave a screaming call that must have sounded pitiful to these five harbingers of death. They scarcely twitched at her defiance. Instead, they watched her with murderous focus. The first lunged forward to bite her. She hopped back off the nest and onto one of the support branches level with the rim, narrowly avoiding the bite. The Jays' attention returned to her squirming babies. The nestlings struggled to raise themselves into an upright stance. Each of them swayed their bobble-heads towards the dark shapes above. They opened their little beaks wide. They had seen the looming shadows of death and innocently expected to be fed.

The female had one more trick up her proverbial sleeve although she hadn't wanted to use it. She called out her alarm chip. A staccato cry. An unending pleading to her babies.

Although they were mostly empty-headed at this helpless young age, deep in their genetic code was etched a recognition for the alarm chip of their parents. An insistent enough alarm call would compel them to wriggle their little bodies out of the nest and down to the hidden protection of the forest floor. Even though they weren't old enough to fledge, they would obey their mother's alarm and maybe, just maybe, they would be obscured in the leaf litter below. The male joined in from farther off. His call was weaker, hampered by pain, blood loss, and distance, but combined it did the trick. The babies slowly made their way to the edges of the nest. The female watched helplessly between her staccato calls. Already she knew this was a mistake. They wouldn't be agile enough to escape the looming Jays. At this point they were just serving themselves up to the predators waiting above.

THUMP THUMP THUMP THUMP

Something large and burly tramped through the forest. It had to be huge. It had to be a mammal. Two of the five Jays turned to look. Whatever it was was growing perilously close with just a few heavy footfalls.

JEER JEEER JEEEER! Whitehead gave a warning call from his high perch. Now all five of the Jays were looking in the direction of the growing noise.

Still the babies meticulously climbed the edges of the nest. The first up teetered on the edge, unsure if it would topple back into the nest or out from it. It didn't help that five nervous Blue Jays stood on the threshold shifting their weight in their indecision. The nestling's little plucked-chicken wings did little to steady it against the precarious rocking.

The female's attention was hopelessly torn between her offspring, the Jays, and this new potential threat. The male hobbled up below her. Their eyes met again. She projected uneasy confidence towards him, and he knew the babies were still alive—at least for the moment. As to the growing thumping, he looked as confused as she did. They kept up the alarm call, for all the good it would do. The combined noise at least appeared to delay the inevitable. The Jays looked at each other, their beaks clacking.

8

THE HUMANS

There were three of them. Gigantic, lanky bipedal monsters come into the domain of Warblers and Jays. Featherless and hairless, with unsightly, lopsided pouches hanging from their backs and wide brims projecting out just above their too-close eyes: they were utterly un-Warbler-like. For a moment, all twelve birds stopped and watched them. The humans exchanged a collection of hushed sounds. One discarded its sack and dug into its contents. None of them could know what the humans would do next. The Blue Jays—thoroughly disturbed by the pained calls of their sibling above, and freaked out by the sudden appearance of humans—took flight high into the canopy. The nest trembled under their combined force and the nestling teetering on the precipice fell backwards into the nest. On its way down it knocked one of its siblings from the low wall and all four of them ended up once again in a pile in the bottom of the nest.

The Jays rose higher and higher into the sky and Whitehead joined its family group. A raucous cacophony of calls followed with them till they disappeared.

The humans had watched the Jay family go before returning to their strange, ritual preparations. Their hushed, nearly subsonic (to a Warbler) vocalizations rumbled amongst themselves. Many long and frightful objects emerged from the sacks on the ground. Long shiny poles. Smaller, handheld devices casting a subtle glow as if illuminated from within. Stacks of thin, white sheets filthy with tiny black markings. Both Blue adults watched, uneasy. Every feather twitched as if to scream out, 'Flee! Flee!'. But between the shock and the injuries, they stayed glued to their nest. After so much, they could not concede now. The nest's once hopeless fate now looked to be an even coin-flip between totally lost and—they dared not think it—somehow spared unscathed.

The humans crept closer and instinct overtook the little Warblers. The male ended up making his way to a high branch and sounding the alarm call again. The female committed herself to a new and impressive broken-wing display. The humans ignored them both, rummaging in the hobble.

At some point during their combined exhausted performances, the humans pinpointed the nest and moved in for a closer look. If the Jays had seemed an overwhelming force, the humans were ten times moreso. It was almost laughable. Still, the female willed her tired, beaten body forward and she flew sideways to try and divert some of the lurking behemoths' attention.

Instead, she found herself caught in an invisible web. Suspended between two of the metal poles she was tangled in the fine mesh hanging there. She wiggled ferociously, paused to catch her breath, found herself even more hopelessly tangled. Trapped in an undignified position, she could only watch as one of the humans approached her. The male looked on helplessly from his high perch.

The humans plucked her out gently and spent the next few minutes engaged in an incomprehensible sequence of behaviors. Later she would think back on the strange abduction trying to somehow connect it to the mystery of her trinkets. But at the time she was very much preoccupied, fluctuating between confusion and her overwhelmed fight-or-flight response. They stretched out her wing and pressed a long metal strip to it. Amidst its cold embrace the female noticed it was notched with tiny markings not dissimilar to those on her ankle trinkets. They blew air on her chest revealing her bald brood patch. They wet her head with a thimble of water and scooted around her soggy headfeathers. She shivered in confusion. Finally they sealed her in a soft, dark bag and set her on what felt like the ground except it was too smooth and hard to be anything in the forest. She fluttered, once, twice. Succeeding only in flipping herself onto her back. Out from the bag she fell. There she lay, slightly dazed, upon an outstretched palm. It took her a moment to collect her wits enough to realize this was her chance to fly away. Even as she catapulted free, it did not feel like escape. It felt like they had grown tired of her for whatever reason and let her go. Humans were exactly as inextricable as the Hermit Thrush had said all those weeks ago.

She flew straight to her nest, fearing the worst. Normally she would dance around and pretend to preen and sing until the creatures moved on, but after the events of today she was possessed by a bitter desperation. She was positive they'd be gone. She could hardly bring herself to look. After all that work, all that fighting. She didn't even know if her mate would survive his injuries. She looked around for him but didn't see him at his high perch. He must have fled when she was captured by the humans. If even one of the babies remained his sacrifice would have been for something.

She peered down into the nest and suffered a completely unexpected shock. Four floundering, wriggling blobs awaited her arrival. They nestlings noticed her immediately, blithely unaware of their collective ordeal. Each of her babies dutifully raised their open maws skyward. She sat dumbfounded on the edge of the nest. *Humans.* When half the forest seemed to want to get her nest—after all that—they hadn't even bothered to eat one nestling. She shook off her funk and descended into the cramped nest. She picked and plucked at her babies: there were no injuries, no blood she could see. They all looked fine.

And then she saw it.

She had grabbed the right ankle of one of the nestlings in her beak and tasted cool metal. The leg dropped from her mouth. She gasped. The baby wiggled its leg randomly about. It was a silvery metal band. A trinket, just like hers. No colored plastic ones, just the one. It caught the light and shone brightly. She checked the others. All four had one. A silvery band on each right ankle.

She had a sudden flashback to her own nestling days. To her mother and their long talks over her trinkets. This great mystery that her mother had dismissed. Claiming that 'some things are not meant to be understood,' when she was especially exasperated at her daughter's incessant questioning. Well maybe she had been right all along. Not in quite the way she had meant at the time, but it was a truth all the same. The realization felt sacred and overwhelming all at once.

The Blue had encountered such essential, unknowable things before. Things totally outside her experience (or evolutionary predisposition). The realization would wash over her and leave her reeling in a primal sensation of the infinite. And in turn, of her own infinitesimal nature. Every time she was forced to turn away lest she become lost in it.

She looked out starry-eyed at the immense possibility. What else was there? What else didn't she know about the world? How many others had bands and for what purpose? She turned away here too and looked at her healthy brood gently begging for grubs beneath her. They had been chosen. Just as she had been chosen. What would she tell them when they were old enough to fledge? What lesson would she leave them with before heading out again to the Caribbean? Was her mate correct, with his bizarre story of good luck charms and glowing bugs? Or was the whole family somehow an unwitting vassal of the humans? Were the humans themselves simple vassals of some greater force, delivering the promise of the trinkets to the chosen? It was an old saying that 'no one could know why a human did anything' after all.

All she knew was simply that she was chosen. Chosen for some purpose, some greater calling. It had guided her for her entire life. And now against all odds, her babies had been spared too because of the same reason. Whatever it was.

All she could do was impress upon them the importance of their lives. The great burden they would carry with them. Sometimes they would be outcast. Chided and hated by others who could only see them as *different*. Few would truly understand. They would rarely see any others like themselves. They also must know that now they were part of an elite company. Those rare few like the grosbeak, like her mate. As far as she could tell, there was something special about each. So she would tell them that they too were special. That they must learn what made them special—learn all they could and seek out others who shared in it. And someday, they must pass along this message to their own nestlings.

The trinkets were goodness incarnate. The idea that the trinkets could be malicious had never once crossed her mind. Even when she was heckled for having them, she did not count them as evil. She knew in her heart of hearts that they were to her benefit. Indeed they were likely to the benefit of all Blues everywhere. She knew the chosen among the Blues were doing something important for the species as a whole. And all she had to do was keep living, keep listening, and keep trying to learn the truth.

9

MIGRATION

The rest of the males had left days ago, but her male was still here. He was recovering from his injuries. His left leg was useless now and he'd never have the agility he once possessed, but he was getting along well enough. It was handy still having him around, she admitted. The nestlings fledged and for a few days they fed them about their territory. Now, days later, the fledglings were flighted and capable of taking care of themselves (if a bit awkward and uncoordinated). Ostensibly, the couple was as free now as they'd been early in the season. Together they hunted like before and fattened up for the long migration ahead. Without his easy agility, the male got the opportunity to show her some of the tricks he'd learned with the Chickadee flock on Noepe. He still managed to nab grubs here and there, and even showed her how to find them hidden inside logs. So there was an intelligence about him.

An evening, a night, and a morning passed and finally the male left. It was not a tearful goodbye, but a simple thing. One moment he was there, and the next he took to the skies. She watched him go. An injured Warbler would face real hardship making it through the winter, especially an aging male. But she knew he had his flock waiting for him and thought there was at least a pretty good chance they'd meet up again next spring. For a few weeks it was just adult females and juveniles patrolling the forest.

She spotted one of her juveniles atop a birch sapling, chasing a spider. The spider walked away in no great rush. It was clear the creature felt slightly molested, but not life-threatened. The juvenile alternated between opening its maw at the spider, and watching it with unfettered curiosity. She worried, watching her juvenile forage, but it looked healthy enough and it still had several weeks before its own departure date. It had inherited a rich enough territory that it could afford to be foolish for a while. She didn't keep track of any of her offspring now that they didn't need to be fed. It wasn't a heartless thing; unlike other species, these juveniles were essentially adults. Fully capable of at least amateurishly fending for themselves. She knew she'd done well for them— against almost literally impossible odds—and reared four healthy Blues into the world.

She wondered if they would take on the social fanaticism of their father or her own private aloofness. It seemed to her that her own mother had taught her to fear and despise her trinkets. And the circumstances of her mate's early life had taught him to cherish them and share them. She herself had taught her offspring (during their feedings) of the weighty importance they carried. She hoped it would not give them an insufferable sense of self-importance. Or perhaps it would make them infinitely curious attainers of knowledge. Perhaps someday a Blue of her own bloodline could unravel the secrets of the trinkets and of the inexplicable behaviors of humans. They could conceivably come into a different personality entirely. No one could know what formative adventures they'd have in the coming weeks, months, and years without their mother to look after them.

The air grew gradually cooler each evening. The Blue puffed her body feathers and huddled in little pockets of warmth each night. Occasionally, she would sleep in her empty nest—which still blocked the wind well and averted any wandering eyes. For the most part she stayed within the territory she and her mate had established. It wasn't necessary, and there would be no consequences for wandering into another Blue's range now, but by this time her sugar maple and its surroundings was like a familiar habit. Her hard-won sanctuary.

Before she left for migration she saw the Blue Jays twice more. Whitehead wasn't with them. Their own young flew with their family group. They were gangly, gray, puffy juveniles squawking insistently at their adults.

The brevity of the sun's arc overcame some threshold deep within her and flipped a biological switch in the Warbler's mind. She too was drawn to the skies. Up, up she climbed into the overcast gray wash above. She started her own migration three grams heavier than she had been when she'd fought off the Jays. Plenty of fuel for her long journey back to the Caribbean. Perhaps she'd see the chivalrous Ovenbird and update him on what she'd learned this season. Tell him of her valiant struggle against six Blue Jays. That would surely set him spinning. Thinking back, it was he who had been the attentive listener. He who had respected her understanding and her eccentricities out of all of them in the flock. Even though she had wholly dismissed him under the spell of the Hermit Thrush's suggestive animosity. Interesting. Though she recoiled at the thought of polite conversation over the countless hours of migration... she wouldn't mind catching up with the Oven, at least for a little while.

While she pondered this, the familiar twisted sugar maple disappeared from view. She flew high, high above the treetops. The impenetrable green tapestry of Abenaki fell away and with it all the thoughts of spring and mating and nesting and predators fell away too. Her mind gave way to that focused zen of migration. Idle chirps collected around her as she rose into the clouds. Dozens of other female Blues took up positions on either side. Each of these little olive ladies had completed her own season full of love and tumult, hope and despair. Some had succeeded, some had failed, most found something in between. Once they hit the coast they would likely join up with other flocks and splinter off, but for now it was a flock of entirely Black-Throated Blue Warblers. The reassuring chips sprung fitfully from everywhere. In the thick cloud cover where their true numbers were greatly obscured, the calls rang out,

"*Are you there? Are you here?*"

"*Who's here? Who's there?*"

"*I'm here! I'm here! Over here!*"

CITATIONS

Birds of the World Citations:

1. Holmes, R. T., S. A. Kaiser, N. L. Rodenhouse, T. S. Sillett, M. S. Webster, P. Pyle, and M. A. Patten (2020). Black-throated Blue Warbler (*Setophaga caerulescens*), version 1.0. In Birds of the World (P. G. Rodewald, Editor). Cornell Lab of Ornithology, Ithaca, NY, USA. https://doi.org/10.2173/bow.btbwar.01

2. Dellinger, R., P. B. Wood, P. W. Jones, and T. M. Donovan (2020). Hermit Thrush (*Catharus guttatus*), version 1.0. In Birds of the World (A. F. Poole, Editor). Cornell Lab of Ornithology, Ithaca, NY, USA. https://doi.org/10.2173/bow.herthr.01

3. Porneluzi, P., M. A. Van Horn, and T. M. Donovan (2020). Ovenbird (*Seiurus aurocapilla*), version 1.0. In Birds of the World (A. F. Poole, Editor). Cornell Lab of Or-

nithology, Ithaca, NY, USA. https://doi.org/10.2173/bow.ovenbi1.01

4.Smith, K. G., K. A. Tarvin, and G. E. Woolfenden (2020). Blue Jay (*Cyanocitta cristata*), version 1.0. In Birds of the World (A. F. Poole, Editor). Cornell Lab of Ornithology, Ithaca, NY, USA. https://doi.org/10.2173/bow.blujay.01

Reference Guide Citations:

5. Sibley, David Allen. 2023. The Sibley Guide to Birds, 2nd edition. *Warbler Taxonomy*. Random House, Inc.
6. Browne, R. & King, D. 2023. Self Editing for Fiction Writers: How To Edit Yourself Into Print. (*Pp 1-224*). William Morrow Paperbacks.

ACKNOWLEDGMENTS

Black-Throated Blue Warbler is my first written piece longer than a short story that isn't a screenplay. I was inspired by the anthropomorphic story Raptor Red by Robert T. Bakker which I read many years ago. I haven't read any other 'animal stories' in years. That story gave me the confidence to write an animal-centric story without resorting to a human perspective to help carry it. I don't know if I'll ever write another story like this. Only you, dear reader, looking back from the future can know if I ever embarked on something like this again.

This particular story possessed my mind for many months. I knew I wanted to get into writing novels and for whatever reason this seemed like the best way in. It grew from several dozen scraps recorded in my phone and on sticky notes every time I found an interesting fact about bird behavior or the research going on in Hubbard Brook.

The idea first came to me when I drove to New Hampshire to pick up my partner, Megan Miller (the illustrator and the one mentioned in the dedication at the beginning of this book) and spent a week there tromping through the Hubbard Brook experimental research forest while they finished out their field season. The scientists there, along with their students from Cornell, were banding warblers to study movement ecology and population dynamics. Shadowing them in their daily efforts, I learned the abysmally low brood success rate due to high predation among other things. Low fledgling success isn't unusual for birds but from a mammal's perspective it was appalling. Of course, if every pair had three successful broods a season, at four fledglings each, then the world would be promptly overrun by warblers.

My first thank you goes to Black-Throated Blue Warbler female I met in person when I was out at the research site. She flew into Megan's mist net. Megan untangled her with the practiced ease of an expert, took her measurements, and let her go. She was healthy, free of disease, and nesting nearby. The nest was perhaps her second brood of the season.

Thank you Megan Miller, for continuing to be a capable Ornithologist whom I can bounce all my terrible ideas off of. I know how challenging it was to find the balance between pure fact and storytelling without accidentally falling into misinformation. I concede many of the best ideas for plot came specifically from your answers to my many, many dumb questions. I will always remember, whatever first idea I might have, nature is vividly more interesting. Thank you as well for your subscription access to Birds of the World where I could double check the specifics of bird weights, measurements, habitat, migration dates, breeding, fledging, diet, coloration, and predation. (Individual articles can be found linked in the citations section.)

And thank you of course for reading so many complete drafts with a discerning eye for comprehension and pacing. In the early days of my writing I did not know anyone else I could turn to for beta reading, and you took the brunt of it. I enjoyed the many long hours we spent discussing how to solve big problems with the story. It may not have looked it since I left our conversations utterly distraught, but I did truly enjoy your unwavering input. You will always be my strongest critic.

Thank you Joni Di Placido, my editor at Page and Proof, for taking the time to learn about warblers and their arthropod prey to fact check some of the claims in my story. You caught lots of little details before I made a fool of myself and you were very gracious in your notes. In the process of line editing and copy editing I learned many interesting quirks about my writing style. There are a lot of pitfalls I regularly trip and fall into. I understand I need to work on these if only to save my editor the headache of identifying all of them in the future.

I also want to note that the acknowledgments section was not reviewed by the editor so any mistakes here are entirely my own.

Thank you Adrian De La Torre for reading several early, unfinished drafts and telling me when you had no idea what was going on. It wasn't until much later that I learned you're supposed to finish a full draft by yourself before sharing it around. Your encouragement and general curiosity helped get this thing out the door much more quickly than if I was beholden to no one but myself. Incidentally, you've been my audience on two subsequent stories I've been working on while BTBW has been in editing. I can always count on you to give whatever vomit draft I hand you an honest scout's try.

And finally a special thanks to the students at Cornell who completed their season of field work. I wrote this story for all of you. Every detail had to be laboriously researched and discussed before it made it into the story. You made this better simply by being good at what you do. I know you love this place and these birds and I hope I captured some semblance of that.

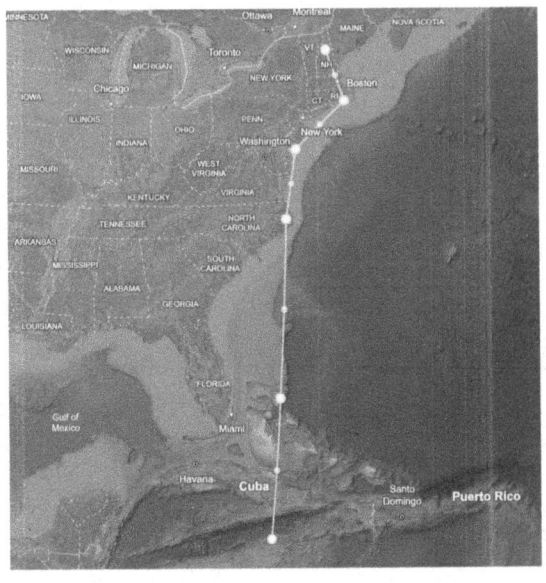

The Black-Throated Blue's migratory path from
Kingston to the White Mountain National Forest.

ABOUT THE AUTHOR

Jordan Spalding is a new author who has been watching birds (birding) for ten years with his partner Megan.

Jordan has been birding all over the United States, Alaska and Hawaii, the Caribbean, Costa Rica, Egypt, Kenya, Tanzania, Mexico, and Peru.

Jordan and Megan have several small parrots at home.

BlueSky - Jpspalding.bsky.social
Instagram - Jordan_spalding_dot_com